Buster Brown's Neighborhood

By Karen Boxell

The Perils of Buster Brown

My name is Buster. My Mister and Missus sometimes add the 'Brown' just to give me more prestige. I kind of like it and it makes a good, full name for an author. As you can see, I'm quite a fine looking fellow. My orange tiger fur is sleek and shiny, and very nicely marked. My eyes are bright and clear-at least they were before the 'event' occurred. (But we'll get to that in due time.) I exercise regularly and have a healthy diet. So, I'm pretty athletic when I work out with my Mister. We have this great toy on a stick. It hangs on a hook in the kitchen, and whenever I go over and sit under it my Mister comes over and trails it over the floor for me to catch. We both love this play time together, and never get tired of this fun game.

Before I came to live in this family I had lived in a cold, dirty cellar in a big city. My mom didn't have a Mister or Missus to take care of her. She was sort of 'on the street'. I had quite a few brothers and sisters, and it was a big chore for mom to look after all of us. Luckily, there was a nice Mister who lived in the building above us, and he would put out some food for mom from time to time. One day he came down to the basement, and, before I knew what was happening, he had scooped me up and put me in a basket, put the basket in his car, and took me for a long ride. At the time I was scared to death, and had no idea what a happy life I was going to.

When I arrived here there were two big guys already in the family. They had come home from Morocco with Missus about eight years ago. At first they weren't very happy to see me. There was a lot of hissing and small growls when I tried to climb up on the bed or the sofa. I pretended I didn't know what they were going on about and just continued doing what I wanted to do. So, it wasn't long before my determination to belong, and my persistence, wore them down. Soon we were all sleeping in a big jumble on the bed with Mister and Missus.

The big top cat was named Sinbad. He deserved to be top cat because he was one really smart fellow. He was white and orange and we looked like we could have actually been related. He quickly became my hero. He ruled the neighborhood, took care of our yard and garden, and wasn't afraid of anything. (But he's a story for another time.)

The other cat was named Voda. He was light brown all over and sort of fluffy. He had some health issues and never went outside. He couldn't find his way home if he got out there. He was a push over though, and had the sweetest disposition of anyone in the family.

For a number of years we all lived happily together in our comfortable old house. Sinbad and I played out in the garden every good day, and in the winter we were all cozy and warm on the sofa with the Mister and the Missus. We always had plenty to eat and we never squabbled about anything.

I wish we could have continued like that forever, but things changed about six years ago. Sinbad got incurably sick. The next year Voda just got too old. They are both together out in the garden under the honey suckle bush. I often go out there and lie down next to them. They are still my big brothers, and I miss them.

So, for the last few years I have been an 'only' cat. My Missus often thinks about getting me a little brother, but when she thinks about how much-trouble and expense a kitten can be, she decides to keep things the way they are. In fact, though I am an 'only', I'm not really alone in the yard and garden. During the day I have a lot of squirrel companions. My Missus puts peanuts out for them to keep them out of the bird food. When I first started going out I tried to catch one of them-just to play, of course. Well, they were really a lot quicker than I was, and I soon gave up trying to catch them when one of them actually ran under my belly, and contented myself with stalking them until they ran up a tree and across the top of the fence.

The big, black crows often come for the peanuts and the bread crumbs Missus puts out. They are too smart for me to sneak up on, and then they screech to tell all the other birds where I am hiding in the shrubs. No fair!

It's at night that my best friends come out to visit. Skunk lives under the deck. She and I have a lot of respect for each other and never have a difference of opinion. Every so often another critter may come into the garden that she doesn't know. That's when she'll let out a little unpleasant order to tell them that our yard is taken and that they had better "move on". She spends a lot of time digging in the grass for some of her favorite food-grubs. I guess she finds many of them because she always seems happy and well fed.

Opossum is also one of my nighttime friends. He doesn't come around as often as Skunk, but when he does I'm always happy to see him. He's a rather quiet fellow-doesn't have too much to say. He looks around to see what might be left to eat under to the tall maple tree where Missus often puts food scraps for all the wild creatures that come to our yard. I think he lived under the garden shed for a while.

Surprisingly, not long ago a wild baby rabbit came to visit. My Missus had commented that she had never thought to see a rabbit in the garden of our city home, surrounded on all side by tall fences and neighbors' houses. Unfortunately, the tiny guy got really frightened when I tried to play with him and brought him into the house. He gave a horrible squeal all scrunched up in the corner by the night stand. Though my Mister and Missus praised me for my prowess, they felt that this little guy was too small to be a playmate for me and needed to go back outside to a much safer place.

I have always enjoyed being out at night taking care of the garden and yard and spending time with some of nature's other critters. However, that all ended this past weekend. Here's what happened.

As usual, I went out after dark and took my usual stroll around the yard to see how things were doing. I have a regular route I like to patrol-just to check on this and that-give a good sniff to see if there is anyone-or thing-new in the area. Things looked pretty normal for most of the night. I went in my private, little cat door a couple of times for a quick snack, before returning to my duties outside.

It had sprinkled a little in the very early morning hours, and the ground was a little damp. I don't know if that is what threw me off guard or not, but something did.

I headed down the driveway to check out the street. I thought I had seen some slight movement just on the street side of a parked car. I was thinking it might be some new neighborhood creature moving in. I wanted to make their acquaintance, and let them know the rules of MY turf. Suddenly ... BLAM!!

Around the end of the car appeared a most fierce apparition-a coyote with a fierce, hungry gleam in his eye. I froze in my tracks. Icy needles ran down my spine. Before I could move a step the coyote lunged for me-no time to turn and run. Instinct wrapped me around his head. My back feet kicked at his chest and tufts of his fur flew to the ground. My claws raked his nose and brow. It stunned him just enough that I was able to jump clear of his vicious teeth and race for the tree by the side fence. Unfortunately, he recovered very quickly and was after me in a flash. I nearly made it to the tree before I felt his hot breath on my ears. I spun around to face him and we had quite a tussle there on the mulch.

I was determined to stay out of reach of those sharp fangs. For a few seconds we had quite a standoff. I was hissing, growling, and snarling. My back was arched, and my fur was fluffed out and standing upright. In a flash I turned and raced down the side of the fence. In my panic I had forgotten about the cement bird bath that was concealed behind the dense yew bushes under the lilac tree. Smack! I hit it full on with my forehead. OUCH! That really hurt. I was seeing stars, and there was two of everything. No time to think about that! I raced across the patio blocks and headed for the back garden with the small pond and the back fence. I almost made it before that awful beast nearly caught me again among the fern. I still don't know for sure how I managed to jump onto the barbeque grill and then over the high back fence. I didn't stop running until I was sure that the wicked creature was no longer on my tail.

I looked around me to find a place to hide-anyplace that was big enough for me and too small for my tormentor. Nothing looked familiar. I didn't know where I was. My head was full of pain, and my eyes were blurry. Then I saw a dark space under a wooden building. I crawled into it as far as I could and curled into a ball, looking back towards the opening through which I had entered. I started to shiver with fright and the aftermath of my race for my life.

It was just beginning to get a little light out. Where was I? How, and when would I get home again? What would my Mister and Missus do when I didn't waken them at 3:30 as usual? Would they be able to find me? How would they know where to look?

I don't know how long I was under that building. I must have slept, or maybe I had passed out. I don't really know. My whole body was sore. My muscles were aching. My head was so painful I could barely lift it. At some point I think I had heard my Mister and Missus calling my name, but I don't know for certain. It was now fully light out. I slowly crept towards the opening of my shelter, sniffing the air for the scent of the horrible demon that had pursued me. I couldn't detect any danger, but my head hurt so badly that I couldn't trust my senses. Inch by inch I approached the light. It hurt my eyes terribly, but I knew I had to get home to my family and safety. I was dazed and confused, not sure which way to go. I had to trust my instincts to take me in the right direction. It was so hard to see clearly, but I had to go on. It didn't matter that I was a mass of hurt from head to toe. I had to get home. My Mister and Missus would be worried sick at my disappearance. I kept putting one foot in front of the other. I don't know how far I had gone, but suddenly I was on a street I recognized. I knew my way home now. I knew it wasn't too much farther. I wished I could go faster, but each step was agony. Even now I can't believe I was able to get over that high fence back into my own yard. How happy I was to be home!

My Mister and Missus were out working in the garden. What a joy to see them! They came to me as I headed for the door. I couldn't wait to get safely inside. Even though I was home, I wasn't sure that the beast was not waiting there to attack me again. I knew I wouldn't have the strength to outwit him a second time. My Mister and Missus followed me inside talking in loving tones and telling me how happy they were to see me. I couldn't tell them how frightened I still was. I showed them by going right upstairs-a place I never spent much time-ever. I just knew I had to get as far away from the evil thing as I could. Upstairs seemed like a good place. There were no doors for the beast to come in.

And that is mostly where I have stayed for the past week. It is quiet up here. The noise from the street is more distant. The light is softer. I do go down to sleep on the sofa with my Mister and Missus when they are home. I have a good appetite, and I have my litter box for the necessity. My eyes are getting better and the headache is mostly gone. I do have a little pain in my right hind leg, but that seems a little better every day. I don't know when I will feel like going outside again. That's okay because I have everything I need right here in the house; a family that loves me dearly, all I could ever want to eat, many comfortable places to rest and sleep, and, when I feel all better, I know my Mister will play with me with my stick toy again.

Rupert Finds a Home

By Karen Boxell

Rupert Finds a Home

Rupert Chipmunk awoke with a start. His head was still sleepy, and he didn't know just why he awoke. Then he knew! His house was going somewhere. How unusual! And Rupert-ready or not-was going somewhere, too.

"Oh, my goodness!" thought Rupert. "I think I am going on an adventure".

He had started looking for a cozy little home last fall before winter came on. The days had turned crisp and sharp, and the nights had become cold and nippy to the nose by the time he found just the right place. And now his snug little house was floating through the air.

Rupert was more curious than frightened. The moving was sort of flowing and gentle-like being rocked in a rocking chair. It was also a soothing way to wake up-if he really **had** to wake up. He yawned and stretched and uncurled from the warm ball he had made of himself.

Just at that moment his house came to a stop, and then it swung a little bit. Rupert held his breath and listened really hard. He could hear two voices talking just outside his house. They were calm and kind sounding voices, voices Rupert knew belonged to Mister and Missus, and Rupert stayed very still listening to them.

After a while, when nothing more happened to his house, he began thinking about how he had found such a wonderfully perfect place to spend the long winter. He thought about the summer. Those were wonderful days. He really hadn't worried about a 'house' then. The days were warm and mostly sunny. The garden was a great place to find things to eat and places to hide from the bigger creatures that also lived in the yard. The lovely colored flowers with their green leaves offered shade as well as a variety of tasty treats. There were lots of seeds to eat under the bird feeders.

Sometimes Mister and a Missus would throw out peanuts in the side yard, and then Rupert would have a real feast. The only problem he had with that was getting them before the big black crows and the squirrels had collected them all.

Oh, yes, and the 'KITTY'. He surely had to keep a sharp eye out for the kitty he had heard Mister and Missus call 'Buster'. Rupert found a little hidey-hole near the side yard where he could watch the activity around the peanuts. He soon realized that he could run a lot faster than the big critters squabbling over the peanuts. They were so busy worrying about each other they hardly noticed him as he raced across the driveway, ran between their feet, grabbed his treasure, and scampered back to his hideout. What a banquet! And there were always enough peanuts to hide away for another day.

And so the summer passed. Autumn came with its golden colors and cooler days. Rupert romped through the falling leaves playing games to which only he knew the rules.

As the days grew shorter and the nights became longer and colder, he knew he had to put aside the fun and frolic, and find a sturdy home for the coming winter. In his adventures through the garden he had seen a number of likely places that just might suit. Now it was time to give these likely spots a better look.

15

The most interesting one was at the bottom of the tree stump next to the outdoor grill. There was a very inviting opening that looked just chipmunk size. Rupert skittered across the back yard, over the rock pile, down the cement slab, and up to the entrance to the little cavern in the tree trunk. It suddenly occurred to him that some other backyard inhabitant may have already claimed this choice spot.

"Hello!" he called out hesitantly. Not a sound came back.

"Anybody in there?" he called out. No one answered.

"May I come in?" he tried once more. Not a word!

Rupert sat down outside the doorway. "Maybe I should just go in," he thought. He had never seen any really dangerous creatures in the garden-except, of course, the 'KITTY'.

And Buster was way tooooo big to fit into this small space. On tip toe Rupert took a step through the doorway. Then another and another.

"Who's there?" a rough, sleepy voice called out.

"What are you doing in my home?" Mr. Mouse stuck his nose out from under his bed of leaves and grasses. "Why are you disturbing us? Don't you know winter is coming? Go away and find your own house!"

"Oh, excuse me Mr. Mouse! I didn't know your family was here, and I DID call out three times before I came in," Rupert explained.

"Well, now you know! Go away and don't bother us again." Mr. Mouse grumpily replied as he settled back into his leafy bed and quickly began to snore.

Rupert backed out of the tree stump, chastened, and a bit disappointed that such a perfect spot was already occupied.

Then he remembered that there was a small hole under the garden timbers that formed the side garden walkway. It didn't take him long to find just the place he had in mind. His little nose twitched as he poked it into the hole and sniffed a big sniff. He didn't want to be taken by surprise like he had been at the tree stump, or embarrassed, either.

"Hmmm," Rupert murmured. "This is a little smaller than I had in mind. It needs a bit of excavating, and I need to have a back door, too."

"Okay," he said to himself. "I'll have to look elsewhere." And off he went to check out the rock pile beside the shed. It was a good sized rock pile and offered a number of interesting crannies to explore. However, upon really close inspection with an eye to move in somewhat permanently, Rupert didn't think it would make a really safe place to stay for the winter. For one thing, there were too many openings to let in cold, windy drafts, and uninvited visitors. For another, the rocks themselves were not very warming for cuddling up to. So, Rupert took himself off to search further.

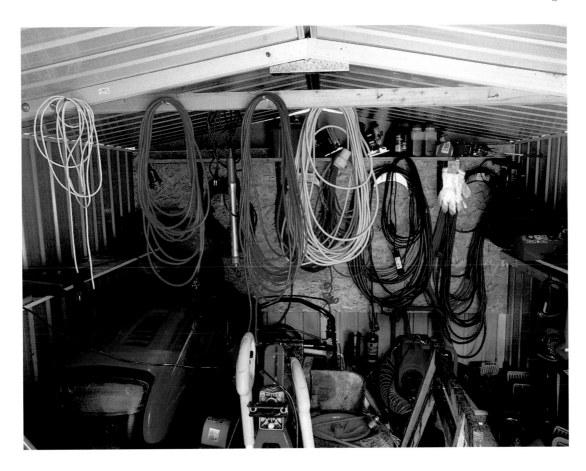

His next stop was at the shed itself. Now this place presented a number of opportunities for winter lodging. It was a lot bigger than one little chipmunk needed, that was for sure. But Rupert had seen Mister and Missus putting things in and taking other things out all year long. He felt confident that inside here he could surely find some suitable spot to spend the winter months. He scurried over to the big door, squeezed under it, and climbed into the shed itself. It was a lot bigger than it had looked from the outside. Rupert stood still and looked all around him. There were so many things in the shed that, at first, he really didn't know where to start looking for just the perfect nook. He sneezed a tiny sneeze and shook his head a little bit.

"Okay," he mused, "I better get busy and see what's here for me."

He wiggled between some plastic cases, and shimmied up the wall post to get a better look around. He spied an old can sitting on a shelf towards the back wall, and went over to get a better look. It was about the right size for him, but it had no top. A short way along the shelf there was a brown box that was a possibility. But when Rupert peered into it, it was already full of stuff, and left no room for him. As Rupert started to climb down to a lower shelf his attention was caught by something bright green hanging right above him. He reached up to touch it and a strand of it fell gently down on his head.

"How soft this is," thought Rupert. "This is what Missus uses to hold up some of the big flowers in the garden. I can make a wonderful bed for myself-if I can only find a good place to make such a bed." And he gazed about him. For a while longer he explored the shed, considering and discarding such things as a flower pot, a worn out garden shoe, a rusty watering can, and a smelly, moldy basket. He had nearly lost hope of finding the perfect place for his winter home, when his wandering eyes came to rest on an adorable little blue bird house.

It was hanging on a hook on the other side of the shed. He didn't remember seeing this bird house out in the garden, but, of course, he didn't climb the trees, so he wouldn't have had the opportunity to see such a thing. He quickly scrambled down from his perch, scurried across the floor, and nimbly climbed up to this remarkable find, hoping no one had already claimed it as their own.

"Hello! Any one in here?" he called as he carefully poked his head into the opening. No one answered, and no one was to be seen inside. Rupert's little heart thumped with delight. He had found the most wonderful house before anyone else had. It could be his for the taking. And he was taking it. He brought some of the soft green material, shredded it carefully, and lay down in his very own bed, in his very own home to sleep out his first long winter.

Now it was spring. Even in his sleepy state Rupert had begun to sense the warming weather. He had been preparing to wake himself up, and now, someone had done it for him in a very nice way. He yawned a few more times, rubbed his eyes, and stretched a big stretch. Just as he was getting ready to peek out the door of his little bird house, it started to move again-as smoothly and easily as before, swinging as it went. Then it started to move upward. Now this Rupert had to see. He had never in his life been up very high.

Suddenly a gentle finger probed the soft material of his bed. A quiet voice wondered. "What is this doing in the bird house? How did it get in here?"

Rupert slowly stood up, put his little feet on the edge of his doorway, and very cautiously peered out. Imagine his surprise to find himself face to face with Missus. She was surely as surprised as he was, and couldn't help but smile into his sleepy eyes.

"Well! Hello there little guy! I can't hang you up high in this tree, can I? How would you ever get down?" and Missus carefully set Rupert's house down between the tree and the back fence in such a way that the KITTY wouldn't be able to disturb him.

Rupert knew that he was a very lucky chipmunk to have found such a house for his own and, that it was in such a yard as that of Mister and Missus-and even Buster.

Jocko Gets Rescued

By Karen Boxell

Jocko Gets Rescued

"Caw. Caw, Caw", sounded from the thrashing branches of the tall maple tree along the back fence.

"Caw, Caw", Jocko called back weakly from the bushes along the side fence. He had been down here all by himself for what seemed an awfully long time. He was getting wetter and wetter, and colder and colder. He didn't really remember exactly how he had ended up in these bushes in the first place. All he could easily recall was that he and his family had left the nest together. It was to be his first venture beyond the tree and nest in which he had been born.

"Caw, Caw, Caw, Caw", was more insistently repeated from above.

Jocko did his best to answer, but all that came out was a raspy, "caw-aw-aw", that he didn't think his parents could even hear.

This crow conversation had been going on for some time this cold, rainy, windy morning in Mister and Missus back yard. Mister and Missus were very used to the calls of the Black Jack crow family, and they knew that the family lived nearby. The birds of the Black Jack family were very familiar with Mister and Missus, and the 'Buster' kitty, too. Members of the family had been frequent visitors to their trees and side yard for the past year. It seemed someone in the family was always on the lookout for the bread bits, peanuts, and other morsels that Mister and Missus regularly strewed about for the wild critters

that lived in the area. The members of the Black Jack family were usually the first on the scene and got the best-and most of-the treats.

However, there had been no treats this morning. Missus knew that the rain would quickly dissolve the bread bits into a sloppy mush that the crows wouldn't be able to pick up and carry off. For that reason she had not put anything out in the side yard.

The longer the crow calling went on, the more concerned Missus became. There surely must be something very unusual going on for the crow family to be so noisily vocal this morning. Mister and Missus had looked out the windows towards the side fence, but the lilac trees were in the way and they couldn't see anything out of the ordinary.

Missus was just thinking about putting on her raincoat and boots to go out and investigate when a visitor stopped by. The visitor was a tall fellow already dressed for the unpleasant weather outside. When Missus explained what was happening the visitor immediately headed to the back yard. At the same moment a pitiful "Caw" was heard from under the shrubbery. This was followed by the shaking of some of the small branches. As the visitor approached the trembling bush Jocko peeked over the greenery. He looked at the visitor. The visitor looked at him.

"Well, hello there young fellow! What seems to be the trouble?" queried the tall visitor.

Jocko wasn't sure if he had seen this person before. After all, he had barely left the family nest and didn't have much experience in the neighborhood yet. Jocko hunkered down under the bush hoping the visitor would just go away.

But that isn't what happened. The visitor parted the bushes above Jocko's head and reached down to pick him up.

"You sure are a bedraggled looking little guy. Come on! Let's get you inside where you can get dry and warm." The visitor spoke in a soothing, comforting voice, and gently lifted Jocko out of the dead leaves behind the shrubbery. Jocko was just too cold, wet, and tired to put up any struggle. In a certain way, he actually felt happy to be rescued by this soft speaking visitor. The visitor tucked Jocko firmly against his jacket and headed into the house to show Mister and Missus what he had discovered.

"Oh, you poor little critter," Missus exclaimed, as she tenderly swaddled Jocko in a warm, fluffy towel. The visitor and Mister helped Missus check Jocko all over to see if he was hurt in any way. His wings and his legs seemed to be in good order as Missus gently patted him as dry as she could. Mister had gone upstairs to fetch the all-purpose cage that was kept handy for any critter emergencies. Missus layered some more towels in the bottom of the cage before lowering Jocko softly down into the cuddly nest.

"I think we should set Jocko up on the dryer in the laundry room, and shut the door" Missus said. "Buster may get curious and come to investigate our little guest. But if Jocko is in the laundry room, he will be safe, and it will be quiet. He needs a little time to dry off and settle down. I think this may have been his first flying adventure and his wings have just gotten too wet and heavy for him to flap. His family is still calling to him, and he will be able to hear them from the laundry room." Missus put a handful of peanuts into the cage with Jocko, and Mister carried the cage and its latest occupant carefully into the laundry room.

While all this had been going on Jocko had lain quietly in the towel. He wasn't afraid. He was actually feeling sleepy and warm. The voices floating around him were peaceful and calming. He could still hear his family calling to him from outside, and that was very comforting, but he didn't have enough energy to answer them right now. As the door closed behind Mister, and Jocko could no longer see any of the people, his eyes closed and he nodded off to sleep in the quiet of the laundry room.

It was some time later before Jocko awoke. At first he didn't know where he was. He certainly wasn't in the family nest swaying in the tree tops. Then he remembered. He was in a cage in the laundry room in the home of Mister and Missus. He hopped to his feet and looked around. That's when he spied the peanuts on the towels next to him. Peanuts are among his most favorite treats. Yum, Yum! Jocko reached out with his beak and took a peanut off the towel. His parents had already shown him how to split open the shell to get the crunchy nut inside. Jocko didn't waste any time gathering all the peanuts and gobbling them down.

"Now what?" he thought. He could hear his family still calling to him from the trees outside. He didn't answer them because he didn't think they would be able to hear him from inside the house. He also didn't want to alert the 'Kitty' to his presence.

It wasn't long before the door to the laundry room slowly opened and Missus looked in. "Oh, so you are awake," she softly said. "And you look like you are ready to rejoin you family. I see you have eaten your peanuts so you are feeling pretty good, I think. The rain has nearly stopped and the wind has died down quite a lot. Your wings look nice and dry. I bet you are anxious to try them out again, aren't you?"

Missus called to Mister to come and see how alert Jocko was. She said she thought it was time to carry the cage outside, and see if Jocko was able to fly up to his family. She knew they were eagerly awaiting his return to the group.

Mister and Missus gently picked up the cage. They slowly and carefully carried it through the kitchen and out the back door into the garden. They could see Jocko's parents and the rest of his family high up in the old maple trees. They could also hear them cawing to Jocko, and they could feel his strong desire to be set free and fly. They gently set the cage on the grass, and lifted the lid on the cage. That was what Jocko had been waiting for. Without any hesitation he spread his wings, lifted into the air and soared straight up onto a sturdy tree limb.

Oh, how happy he was! Not only was he back with his family, but he could fly!

And his family was overjoyed to have him back with them. It had been an anxious morning for them. It had been a long, tense wait for them. But, finally they were reunited. Jocko was home, and all was right in their world.